THE Ellie McDoodle DIARIES

The Show Must Go On

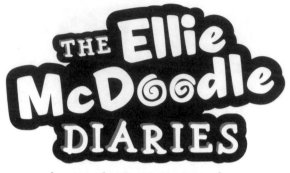

THE Ellie McDoodle DIARIES

by Ruth McNally Barshaw

THE Ellie McDoodle DIARIES

The Show Must Go On

WRITTEN AND ILLUSTRATED BY

Ruth McNally Barshaw

BLOOMSBURY

NEW YORK   LONDON   NEW DELHI   SYDNEY

For all who paint on a smile and keep going in tough
times, especially Marilyn, Lee, Heidi, and Mom

First published in the United States of America in May 2013
by Bloomsbury Children's Books
www.bloomsbury.com

For information about permission to reproduce selections from this book, write to
Permissions, Bloomsbury Children's Books, 175 Fifth Avenue, New York, New York 10010
Bloomsbury books may be purchased for business or promotional use. For information on bulk
purchases please contact Macmillan Corporate and Premium Sales Department at
specialmarkets@macmillan.com

Library of Congress Cataloging-in-Publication Data
Barshaw, Ruth McNally.
Ellie McDoodle : the show must go on / written and illustrated by Ruth McNally Barshaw. — 1st U.S. ed.
p. cm.
Summary: When Ellie McDoodle signs up to help with her school's production of
The Wizard of Oz, she gets more than she bargained for as she helps paint sets, plan
costumes, and cast the show, which leads to her first big fight with best friend Mo.
ISBN 978-1-61963-059-8 (hardcover) • ISBN 978-1-61963-060-4 (e-book)
[1. Theater—Fiction. 2. Schools—Fiction. 3. Best friends—Fiction. 4. Friendship—Fiction. 5. Family life—Fiction.]
I. Title. II. Title: Show must go on.
PZ7.B28047Els 2013   [Fic]—dc23   2013003639

Typeset in Casino Hand
Art created with a Sanford Uni-ball Micro pen
Book design by Yelena Safronova

Printed and bound in the U.S.A. by Thomson-Shore Inc., Dexter, Michigan
2 4 6 8 10 9 7 5 3

All papers used by Bloomsbury Publishing, Inc., are natural, recyclable products
made from wood grown in well-managed forests. The manufacturing processes
conform to the environmental regulations of the country of origin.

As Mom hands me Henry's leash she says with great drama, "Ellie, will the first act of your day be comedy or tragedy?"

I think she's been watching too many movies lately. Still, I know what she wants to hear, so I recite my lines: "Don't worry. I'll make Henry pretend to be a good dog." I'm kidding. He's usually good.

Mom applauds. "Hurry back for breakfast!"

Ten minutes later the leash yanks from my grip.

Sweet, plodding Henry becomes the world's most determined squirrel hunter. The three of us race across lawns, around trees, through a sprinkler.

Luckily, I manage to dodge the first shower.

The second shower sprays me.

It soaks Mrs. Hamilton.

Wait—where did she come from?
She screams:

BAD DOG!!! GO HOME!!!

My poppies!

SORRY!

trail of uprooted flowers

Henry and I exit, fast.

I arrive home to this scene.

Sometimes I think my family is auditioning for Wackiest Family of the Millennium.

Risa's getting good at playing ukulele.

"Stinking, inking little Ellie,
Sweating, fretting, wet and smelly."

Cheezers.

Artist Mom

Ellie, your color isn't good. You're 40% crimson with a tinge of hunter green. Are you feeling queasy? Let's get you some ginger ale.

WOOF-WOOF!

Ben-Ben is a dog?

I wolf down breakfast and head to school.

On the walk to school, my friends have simple advice about that mean old witch, Mrs. Hamilton.

Daquon: Don't walk your dog past her house. Then he can't go in her garden.

Travis: Have a heart-to-heart talk with her.

Ryan: No! Fight! Be brave!

I'm glad when we're interrupted by Mo. There's a good reason she's my best friend.

"This is it. My life is complete. Follow me."

Mo is sooo dramatic.
She practically drags me to see . . .

> # 6th Grade Play: The Wizard of Oz
> Auditions tomorrow!

Mo needs to be Dorothy.

Do you realize how many pairs of red shoes I have?
What do you want to be?

I want to paint the sets!

Visions of giant Munchkinland flowers and cute little mushroomy cottages spring up in my brain.

The bell rings and the school day starts, but we're too excited to think about anything but the play.

Our English and history teacher, Mrs. Whittam, calls our class to attention.

Mrs. Plassid will tell you more about the play soon. Right now, let's focus on the Industrial Revolution. We're making robots.

You mean tin men?

Tin man or electronic woman, make it a marvel.

She passes around a sample.

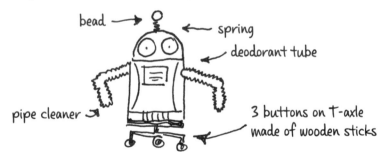

bead → ← spring
deodorant tube
pipe cleaner ↗
3 buttons on T-axle made of wooden sticks

It's due in two weeks. We start with scrap box body parts:

♪♫ Robot techno music plays, giving us inspiration. ♫♪

Yasmeen

This is the perfect robot head and body! Plus it has a unicorn horn!

Scrap Box

This already looks like a bird!

Roarrr!

← Ryan's robot

The box is emptied so fast I barely get a look inside. I invite Mo, Travis, Yasmeen, and Daquon to come to my house tonight to make robots.

After history class, we're ushered into the auditorium. Mrs. Plassid, the reading teacher, reveals her big plans for the play:

- The whole sixth grade is involved.
- We'll have many important crew positions; not everyone will be on stage.
- We can submit artwork for a chance to see it printed on the cover of the program booklet.
- Our Oz production will feature music by the high school orchestra. It's a musical!

Crazy, chaotic music fills the auditorium—
25 different songs at once. And, um, it doesn't
sound good. This is what I hear:

Ha! This will be fun!

The whole school is excited about the play—
even the cafeteria crew gets in on the act.
Today's lunch:

Dorothy Gale Farm Milk

Yellow Brick Corn Bread

Cyclone Veggie Sticks

Talking Tree Applesauce

Cowardly Chicken

We talk about the Oz movie.

Daquon: Explain this. Lion wants courage, Tin
Man wants a heart, Dorothy wants to go home,
and all Scarecrow wants is to
be clever as a gizzard?

Me: What is a gizzard?

Daquon: It's a bird's second
stomach. It grinds food.

gizzard

Ryan: My brother is clever as an elbow.

Travis: I want to be clever as a forehead—four
heads are better than one!

Mo is totally obsessed with Oz. She can't stop talking about the play. During science class she borrows my red marker.

Mo: Ta-daa! Ruby slippers!

Me: You know, the shoes in the Oz book are silver, not ruby.

Mo: Really? I like the movie better than the book. I never read the book.

Me: Then how do you know you like the movie better?

Mo: Because ruby slippers look good on me.

I take a break from drawing storm clouds to make a surprise for Mo.

Dorothy

Toto too

Mrs. Hamilton

Maybe I'm getting sort of Oz crazy too. Visions for set design—not only painting—start flooding my brain.

Like this one: How do we make the Munchkins in our play seem to be two feet shorter than the other characters?

My answer: put the yellow brick road on stilts.

Ramp hides stilts from the view of the audience.

Dorothy and witches stand here.

Munchkins gather here.

Shoes are attached to their knees.

After school I show Mrs. Plassid my plan.

Her classroom looks like a shrine to <u>The Wizard of Oz</u>.

Mrs. Plassid says, "I want you to be the stage manager. Analyze the show and make suggestions for improvement—costumes, script, music, props, every single part of it."

Wow. I tell her a bunch more ideas that I think of right there on the spot. Her smile fades. Maybe she isn't as big an Oz fan as I thought?

She says, "Write down every <u>good</u> concept and show me the best ones later."

No problem! I'll think up a million more!

When my friends gather at my house to work on robots, I tell them my big news. "Guys, you'll never guess: I am the new STAGE MANAGER!"

They all think it's cool, but Mo gives her special overreaction, which I love:

ELLIIIIEEEE!!!!

Mo is the best happy-screamer ever.

What does the stage manager do?

Nobody knows. I say, "I manage everything onstage. And my first official act is—drumroll, please—"

I give the role of Dorothy to Mo. No audition is necessary, I tell her. Everyone cheers. Mo beams. Then she makes an acceptance speech. Then she screams again. Yasmeen asks if anyone is nervous about auditions tomorrow. Turns out <u>everyone</u> is nervous—maybe that's normal.

Then we start working on our robots.

Yasmeen: We should form a secret club with just us five.

Travis: What would we do in it?

Daquon: Hang out together.

Me: We could play games!

Mo: We need a name.

We all agree, so we think up some:

Mo: TEMDY—our initials!

Me: Five Fantastic Friends For Fun—FFFFF.

Daquon: Five of Epic Sagacity—that's wisdom.

Me: FOES. Ha!

We all like that name.

Josh peeks in.

Josh: Groovy Oblivious Oz Fans Slacking. GOOFS. Ha!

Me: FOES it is. Go away, Josh.

Josh doesn't leave. He hangs around while we make our robots.

You should make it do stuff.

He DOES.
My robot hooks onto things, he has a secret compartment that opens to reveal his inner workings, he rolls, and he leaves a trail of thread.

No—I mean lights and motors.

Bleah. I like it the way it is right now.

Later that night Mom and Dad set up a Wizard of Oz party for our family to watch the movie.

Wow—our kid is the stage manager!

I tell them the high school orchestra's playing all the music. It'll be Risa on flute, Josh on tuba, and Risa's boyfriend, Peter, on cello.

Go, Team McDougal!

I'll be honest, <u>The Wizard of Oz</u> gave me nightmares when I was little—especially the tornado. I ask my family to name the scariest parts.

Mom: The flying monkeys.

Dad: Auntie Em turning into a witch in the crystal ball.

Risa: The ruby slippers because they stood for blood and sacrifice.

Eww. They do not. Moving right along . . .

Arf, arf!

Peter: The Tin Man. That heartless man with an ax gives me shivers.

Josh's: The ending! What if life really <u>is</u> only a dream? Frightening!

The next morning at school our auditions team meets:

Mrs. Plassid, show director

Mrs. Ping, my school principal

Mrs. Evans, high school choir teacher

Mr. Cornelius, high school orchestra director

Me

I tell them I saved some time and already made Mo Dorothy. I expect them to be glad, but they frown!

Mrs. Plassid says something that sends icy shivers up my spine: "Mo might not be the best choice. We'll see how it goes."

Audition number 1: Ryan.
He's jittery at first.
Mrs. Plassid says, "Breathe."
Ryan's trying out for Tin Man, but he'd make a better Cowardly Lion! I write my comments on little cards. We're not allowed to speak.

Mo is the first of 37 Dorothys. Her acting is brilliant! I applaud. Mrs. Plassid stops me. Then Mo sings. Mrs. Evans looks down. Mrs. Ping frowns. Mo finishes. I let out my breath, slumping like a saggy, deflated balloon. Maybe Mo could take singing lessons.

We sit through the rainbow song 36 more times—also 3 Lions, 7 witches, a wizard, 2 Scarecrows, 3 Tin Men, 6 Lullaby League ballet dancers (all good), 3 Lollipop Guild guys, and a flying monkey who bounces around scratching his armpits. "Ooo—eee—eee!"

For the last audition, Nikki takes the stage. She looks like Dorothy. When she belts out "Over the Rainbow," my mouth hangs open. She's perfect. Wait—MO WAS BETTER.

When Nikki leaves the stage our audition team moves to the teachers' lounge to talk about the actors.

I'm in the teachers' lounge!!!!!

I'm surprised—it's not much of a party room. There's a long table with about 20 chairs, some cupboards, and a sink. It's kind of boring.

Someone: Nikki is Dorothy.

Me: Wait, what?

Them: Absolutely. It's a no-brainer. Yes.

Me: What about Mo for Dorothy?

Them: I don't think so. I'm afraid not.

Me: But she could work on it!

Them: Ellie, Nikki has a beautiful voice.
Mo will do better with a non-singing role.
Nikki is Dorothy. Nikki. Nikki. Nikki.
Okay, who for the Wicked Witch of the West?

I barely hear the rest of the discussion. What happened here? My mind is racing. Maybe Nikki was a better Dorothy, but Mo will be incredibly hurt. She will be crushed. She's desperate to be Dorothy. This is awful! Horrible! Disastrous!

How will I break the bad news to her?

Mrs. Plassid bursts into my thoughts.

Good job, everyone. Now don't forget, this is top-secret information until tomorrow. No telling. Got it, Ellie?

Got it.

Don't tell anyone? That means I have to avoid all people until tomorrow morning.

The school bell rings as our meeting ends. I hide in the custodian's closet until the school is quiet.

Then I sprint home, unseen.

But as soon as I start to relax,

Ringggg!
Ringggg!
Ringggg!

Risa: Why didn't you answer the phone? It's for YOU! It's Mo! Take it!

Me: No! I'm not here!

To make it true, I leave.

I feel like a tornado's chasing me. I run as fast as I can to the woods.

There are no phones here and nobody asking questions or making me keep a secret I don't want to keep. I can think and breathe, finally.

Maybe Mo won't be that sad. Maybe it's not such a big deal. Maybe I am worried about nothing! Yeah, right. I know exactly what this means to her. It's huge. And she's going to hate me.

Why did I promise her the Dorothy role?

What am I going to do about it now?

1. Panic.
2. Cry.
3. Throw up.
4. ?

Dorothy gets a happy ending. Does Mo? Do I?

Mom says when I'm off balance, start with simple stuff.

1. Yoga breathing.
2. What's here around me.

- o I see: birds, glittery river water, trees
- o I hear: tweeting and chirping, rushing water, jumping fish
- o I smell: GREEN. That's silly. Can green be a smell? I smell flowers plus tree leaves plus thick rich dirt—a little sweet and a tiny bit fishy.
- o I taste: Hmm. I'll pass.
- o I feel: the wind blowing from the southwest

Sunfish zip through the blue water like birds across the sky. If sunfish could fly, what kind of wings would they have?

This makes me think about other animals. How would a black rhino fly? Or a pig? Or a monkey? Flying monkeys . . . the ones in the movie look like creepy bellboys in a haunted hotel. We get to design our own costumes for the show. How do I want our flying monkeys to look?

winged monkey

superhero cape

jet pack

magic carpet

Ben-Ben the monkey boy

Woof!

I'm going home to redraw these. I can't wait to show them to Mrs. Plassid tomorrow!

As I leave the woods a branch smacks me in the face. Ouch. But it's worse when I'm smacked again at home, because it's reality hitting me. How did I manage to forget about Mo for an hour?

Mom: Did something happen between you and Mo?

Me: She wants the part of Dorothy really bad, but they're making her the witch instead. And I'm not allowed to tell her.

Mom: Oh boy.

Ben-Ben: Woof!

Mom: Mo will understand.

Risa: Well, don't say or do anything stupid and you'll be fine.

Gee thanks, Risa. That's so incredibly NOT helpful.

Mo shows up at school the next day in costume. She's in a DOROTHY COSTUME. I want to crawl under a rock.

The entire school gathers at the front doors.

Everyone cheers when Mrs. Plassid and Mrs. Ping arrive with the lists and some tape. Cheezers. Do they have to make such a big production of it?

The crowd pushes toward the doors. I'm about ready to faint.

"Mo, I—"

But she doesn't hear me. I hold my breath while Mo walks up to the list, looks at it, and looks at me.

Mo, they—

No! I'm not here!

She runs. I follow but she loses me.

When I get to class, the big topic is the cast list. I don't say anything. I keep watching the door. No Mo.

Three hours later Mo finally comes into the lunchroom. She's wearing all black. I rush to hug her but she takes a step back. Whoa. This is like Alternate Universe Mo.

Me: Are you okay?

Mo: Why do you care?

Me: I—wha—I—I—saved you a seat, over there.

Mo: No thanks.

She walks to my table but for the first time since we met, Mo chooses a seat away from me.

The whole rest of the day she ignores me.

After school, I show my monkey-costume ideas
to Mrs. Plassid. She says they're good. Maybe she
says something more about them. I don't know.
I'm thinking about Mo and trying not to cry.

I walk home alone.

When I get to my front porch I stop and sniff—
dinner! Lasagna and garlic bread—my favorite. I
hear music. I open the door and then—

FREAKOUT!!!!

Something rushes at my knees!
Glowing eyes!
Screechy voice!
Something pointy!
What is it?!

"Fall back, mortal girl!"

I jump back, screaming. I'm still on my tippy toes when I hear Josh's evil guffaw. After he stops laughing his head off, Josh gives me a crash course in robotics for Mrs. Claus. (She's a reject from Mom's Santa statue collection. She tends to show up unexpectedly!)

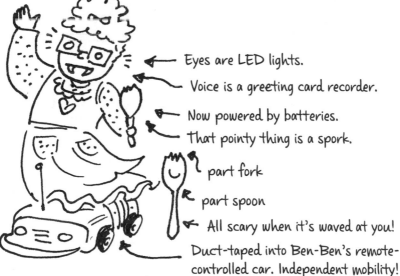

Eyes are LED lights.

Voice is a greeting card recorder.

Now powered by batteries.

That pointy thing is a spork.

part fork

part spoon

All scary when it's waved at you!

Duct-taped into Ben-Ben's remote-controlled car. Independent mobility!

Josh says I could do some of this with my robot for class. I don't know. It looks complicated.

He offers to help, but I can't concentrate.

I decide to call Yasmeen to help figure out what to do about Mo. Yasmeen says I should apologize.

Maybe she's right.

I try calling Mo's number. She doesn't answer, and I don't want to leave a message because I don't know what to say.

The next day Mo isn't at school. I'm about to ask the FOES what they think when suddenly Travis gets all dramatic.

Travis: If I tell you who I like, will you keep it a secret?

Me to myself: Whoa. Is it Mo?

Yasmeen: Yes! Tell us!
Travis (whispering): Sitka.

Me to myself: Why Sitka?

Yasmeen: She's lovely.
Travis: Yeah, definitely.
Daquon: She's smart in math.
Me: She sits at my science table. I like her, but sometimes she kind of takes over.

Oops. That might not have been the right thing to say.

I add quickly: She's cool, Travis.

In English class Mrs. Whittam gives us a new assignment. We each choose three minutes from the Oz movie to remake somehow in a different art form. We can do dance, art, a song, a comic strip, whatever we want. In a few weeks we'll watch each one in order. It'll be like seeing the whole movie from start to finish, except all artsy-ish.

What do I want to do for my scene? I have no idea.

Puppet show?

Painting?

Diorama?

Of course there's an excited rush for scenes. While I'm considering all the possibilities, everyone else hurries to claim their favorite three minutes. One card shoots up out of the tangle of people, flutters down, and lands on my toes. It says:

> Dorothy and Toto get picked up and whisked to the castle by winged monkeys.

I try to put it back on the table, but Mrs. Whittam stops me. She says no returns. I'm stuck with this card! I didn't even pick it!

This card picked me.

Grr.

I could have a million good designs for EVERY OTHER SCENE in the movie except this one. This is so unfair.

After lunch the whole sixth grade meets for the First Read. That's where all the characters read through the official Wizard of Oz script out loud, together, each one saying his or her own part. I'm glad to see that Mo shows up for this. Maybe I can talk with her after.

First Read is awesome. It's perfect. You can almost feel the electricity around us. Even Mo is fantastic.

I know she'll be the best witch ever.

Our main characters:

Nikki = Dorothy
Daquon = Scarecrow
Travis = Tin Man
Ryan = Cowardly Lion
Sitka = Good Witch Glinda
Mo = Wicked Witch
Jamian = Wizard

Some of our crew:

Luci = sound and lights
Rachel = costumes
Glenda = publicity

I'm stage manager, and I have no clue what that means anymore.

Mrs. Plassid tells me at the end of First Read that we'll spend the rest of the rehearsals trying to recapture today's energy and excitement.

Next, Mrs. Plassid announces a surprise: mentors!
Drama students from the university are here
to work with us one-on-one to help with our roles.
Each kid has a mentor.

My mentor: Zac

huge eyes

funny

cutest guy ever

duct tape
bracelet?

rubber
chicken?

I totally scored.
He's the BEST.
Zac tells me the duties of a stage manager.
- Follow the director everywhere.
- Take copious notes on everything she says.
  - Find out the definition of copious.
  - Never mind, Zac tells me it means LOTS.
- Give cues to the actors so they know when
  to say what and where to stand, if they
  forget.
- Make sure the props are where they
  should be.

Zac has funny stories about mistakes on stage, like one about a girl in a house scene who couldn't open the front door.

She kept pulling until finally someone behind the door pushed hard, and the whole set wall fell down! It collapsed, right in the middle of a play!

The stage manager was so horrified he stood there with his mouth open, doing nothing.

I add to my list:
- Make sure all the set doors work right.
- Don't get so horrified by anything that I stand there with my mouth open doing nothing.

Everything is going like a happy dream until Zac steps away to take a phone call.

I hear him say, "Nah, you didn't interrupt anything. I've been teaching some little kid about theater. I'm just about done."

Some little kid? Is that what he thinks of me? My cheeks burn. My eyes water. I wipe them fast and sneak away to see what everyone else is doing.

The cast is learning how to be better actors. The lessons are STRANGE. Mrs. Plassid calls out something and everyone acts like what she said.

"Be an apple!"

"Now with a bite out!"

"Show me fear.
Now extreme fear!"

"Show me dull.
Show me super smart!"

"Show me mean.
Heartless. Evil."

"Show me happy."

Mo's eyes crinkle. Her eyebrows go up and her fists clutch together.

"Good! Give me joyful, giddy, the most deliriously happy happification in the universe!"

Mo looks at Sitka and gives her the happiest scream ever. Her whole body lights up. Is she acting or is this real? I don't know. It makes Sitka laugh.

If I were an actor instead of stage manager, I would never have promised Mo that she could be Dorothy. I would be happy right now.

Maybe Mo will let me talk to her at the end of rehearsal. Maybe I'll know what to say.

Mrs. Plassid bumps my elbow while I'm watching Mo. "Ellie, do you have a few minutes to see the sets? Our set crew has been working hard on them."

A couple of kids and parent volunteers show us the cornfield set, where Dorothy meets Scarecrow.

The yellow brick road goes up the wall at an angle, sort of fooling the eye. When it's all painted it'll be even better.

After rehearsal ends, I try to talk to Mo. She leaves too quickly.

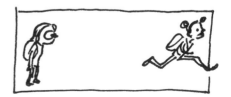

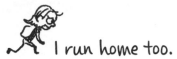 I run home too.
Ben-Ben is happy to see me. He jumps all over me, trying to lick my face.

Dad welcomes me with this:

Hey, sport, I've arranged for a backstage tour of Watson Center next week so you can see how the pros do it. Bring the FOES along. Actually, anyone who wants to can join us.

That'll be GREAT! Mo will love it!

Well, the old Mo would love it. This new Mo might not. I don't know her anymore.

Just then I notice zombies in the living room!

It's Josh and his buddies Iggy and Doof getting ready for Gory Story Fest at the library.

A packet of unflavored gelatin plus a tablespoon of milk makes the most fantastic fake peeling skin ever. Apply. Wait 15 minutes for it to dry.

Josh got the recipe from Risa. It's supposed to clean your face, but it wrinkles up and looks like second skin. I apply some of Josh's wrinkle-making goop.

Wow—instant old lady!

Iggy: Oh—did we forget to tell you? Don't get it on your chin or near your ears or eyes.

Doof: Yeah, it hurts like crazy to peel it off.

Josh: Yeah—water takes it off MUCH easier.

I sure wish someone had told me that sooner.

We should use this in our play! It's ideal for Auntie Em and Uncle Henry! They'll look ancient!

We could use it on the Wicked Witch too. It'd be funny that throwing water on her in the play really would melt her face off! What a neat special effect.

The boys leave. The house is quiet (except for Ben-Ben, who is barking at squirrels).

My thoughts get louder in my head. Josh and his buddies never seem to get mad at each other. I wish Mo was like that with me. I miss Mo.

Suddenly Risa's in my face.

Her: Why are you slobbering?

Me: I've lost my best friend and there's nothing I can do about it.

Her: You can always do something about it.

Me: No! It's over!

Her: Then make art. It'll help you feel better.

Friendship bracelets qualify as art, I think.

First I braid a collar for Ben-Ben, to get him to stop begging. Basically it's a long friendship bracelet.

Then I make two normal-size bracelets:

Best

Friends

Mo can choose the one she likes, and the other is for me to wear. I can't wait until tomorrow!

Now that I'm feeling better, I sneak a peek at what Risa's doing. She says she's creating a piece for an art show at school.

It looks like a rock to me. It's a nice rock, but I don't get how it can be called art.

Maybe it's modern art?

The next day I'm at school early. Mo is with Sitka and Travis. Sitka keeps saying "mayonnaise," and then all three of them laugh like it's the funniest thing ever. It's contagious. I smile. Then I start giggling along with them. Soon I'm laughing hard.

Glenda walks up and asks me what's so funny. I shrug. I'm too embarrassed to say I don't know the inside joke. Glenda looks at me, expecting something. Awkward silence follows. I burst out with this: "I'll help you 'ketchup' later! Ha!"

Nobody even smiles. Quick, I have to say something.

"Look what I made for you!"
I thrust the two bracelets toward Mo.

This next part I swear I will remember until I am a little old lady, all done with living.

Time slows down.

Sitka oohs and ahhs over the bracelets and then picks up both of them.

She ties one on Mo's wrist and starts tying the other onto her own wrist!

In the next instant, THE BELL RINGS!!!!

I am trying to concentrate in class, but it's impossible. I have to get that bracelet back from Sitka. Mo completely ignores me. I don't know how to reach her.

In the afternoon in math class Mr. Brendall tells us to develop a pie chart, a bar graph, and a Venn diagram relating to the Oz play. That's too easy. I have heaps of them.

I can't turn these in as class work.

Instead I turn in boring things like this bar graph:

← How much work I thought the play would be

← How much work it really is

← How excited I am to be stage manager

We have our first rehearsal today. The script is easy to memorize. It helps that everyone knows the Wizard of Oz story.

Mrs. Plassid introduces Toto to us. He's her grouchy old cairn terrier. Nobody wants to pet him. Cheezers. Ben-Ben is a better dog.

Nikki is exactly what we thought she would be: the perfect Dorothy. She's small and meek half the time, and she's great and powerful when the script calls for it.

There's only one problem: Toto doesn't like her, not one bit.

Glinda the Good Witch (Sitka) doesn't like Dorothy either. She keeps "accidentally" poking Nikki with her pointy wand.

I think Sitka is trying to show loyalty to Mo, but it's mean. Plus I don't think Mo likes it.

Daquon says Sitka's merely being true to character. "The 'Good' Witch is bad! She steals shoes from the dead witch. Grave robber! She puts them on Dorothy, making a <u>kid</u> her partner in crime. THEN she makes Dorothy walk miles to Oz instead of giving her a ride in her bubble. She's a wicked Good Witch."

Ha! He's right.

At the end of rehearsal I tell Mrs. Plassid my latest brilliant plan: Make the sets, costumes, and makeup for the first 16 minutes brown and white to match the beginning of the movie. The end could be in color instead of brown, because Dorothy's changed and sees the world differently.

The concept grows while I talk about it. Mrs. Plassid says I have excellent brainstorming skills.

I'm feeling super confident. I find Mo and blurt out:

Those bracelets weren't for you and Sitka. They were for you and <u>me</u>.

Mo listens.
She nods.
She looks me in the eye.
Finally, I've reached her!

Mo unties my bracelet and hands it to me.
No, no, no!
This is not what I wanted.
No.
She leaves.

I have to breathe. I can't think. I can't even walk straight—I fall twice and practically crawl to the woods. I have never felt so alone, but this is the <u>best</u> place to be alone. Except it's occupied.

I watch as Travis and Sitka sit on MY rock and start reading the script together. I sneak away, unseen.

Where do I fit in? Will I ever get my best friend back? Why is everyone all gaga over Sitka? Is there something wrong with me? My head feels like I've been pounding it on my rock.

Somehow I make it home, where Mom takes one look at me and almost suffocates me with a long hug.

⌇Oooooooooof!⌇

While the rest of the family performs their particular weirdness that is them, Mom and I sit. I let it all out.

Mom: Maybe you're trying too hard. Not everything can be fixed.

Me: It HAS to be! I've never had a best friend like her before. I can't lose her. I have to talk to her. But I don't know what to say.

Mom: The right words will come at the right time.

Oooo-Oooo-Oooo-Oooo-Oooooooooooo!

Risa and Peter perform a ukulele duet of "Over the Rainbow," Hawaiian style.

Ah-wooooo!

Ben-Ben scratches imaginary fleas.

Booooo! I'm going to get youuuuu!

Josh is remote-controlling a ghostly Mrs. Claus.

Dad's putting dinner on the table.
He sniffs the chicken.

"Ooooo! I'm a good cook!"

I almost smile.
Mom hugs me again.
"Let's put this on the
back burner for now.
Time to eat."

Okay. I'm all cried out.
I don't feel like eating, though.

63

At the table Josh brings up tornadoes.

Josh: I've been thinking about how you could handle the tornado scene for your play.

Me: Mrs. Plassid wants to project video of a tornado onto the farmhouse set.

Josh: Well, that would work, but what if instead you made a giant remote-controlled tornado that could move around the stage?

He sketches it.

person on the catwalk by the ceiling

fishing pole

fishing line

spring covered with gray cloth

race car disguised as a dust cloud

miniature Dorothy house and barn

me, kind of in awe

Josh has more plans:

giant ceiling fan

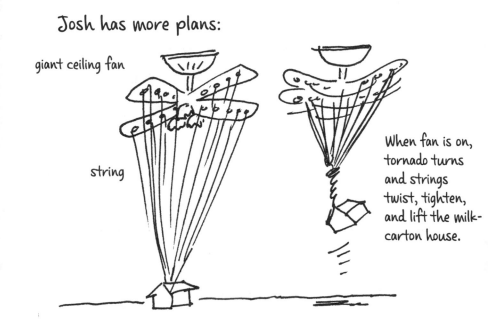

string

When fan is on, tornado turns and strings twist, tighten, and lift the milk-carton house.

For the next hour we all brainstorm tornadoes.

I'm really lucky to have my family.

In class the next day Mrs. Whittam announces that some students are ready to show off their robots in today's Radical Robot Reveal.

Most of the robots don't do anything except look cool.

One is TOTALLY INSPIRED. It has a motion detector that makes it flash lights and play a siren. It's called a Body Odor Detecting Robot.

That means you smell! Ha-ha-ha.

This makes me want to do a really good job on mine. I might need Josh's help after all.

I notice at lunch that Travis is wearing my bracelet that Sitka took.

I don't know whether to cry or laugh about it, so I decide to laugh about that and about everything else today. I try to be my funniest self. I get everyone to rate today's cafeteria food on a scale of 1 to 10.

Here's what we agree on:

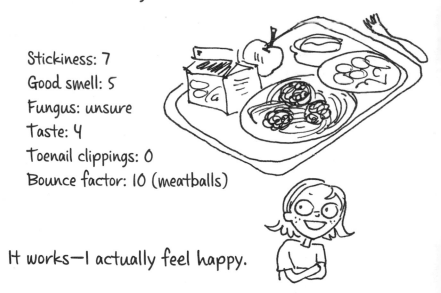

Stickiness: 7
Good smell: 5
Fungus: unsure
Taste: 4
Toenail clippings: 0
Bounce factor: 10 (meatballs)

It works—I actually feel happy.

In rehearsals, Mrs. Plassid is the Queen of Keep Everyone Busy.

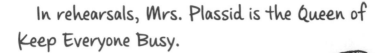

Everyone who isn't a Munchkin, a witch, or Dorothy, listen up. See this? Dozens of these hang from the Enchanted Trees and get thrown at Scarecrow and Dorothy. Guess what you're making for the next hour?

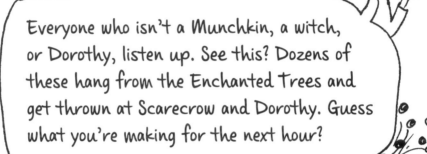

Mo makes two, even though as a witch she's excused. Then she gets called to rehearse her part, and I go over to watch.

Mo's character comes across as sad, not wicked. I don't know if that's on purpose.

I hope Mo starts to have fun being a witch. Her costume isn't made yet. Maybe I can draw something she'll like.

We might have a prop of some sort to make her costume even better. I decide to check the props box.

That's when I find the chicken.
There's a note attached!

To Ellie:

You ran off before I had a chance to tell you.
Some theaters have weird traditions.
You should start one in yours. On campus
we always have a rubber chicken that
appears in the last night's show. The
director isn't in on it—only the cast decides
how it'll make its entrance.
    I'll be watching for Rubber Chickie!

Your favorite mentor,
Zac

WOW. I feel honored. He isn't treating me like
a little kid anymore. Zac is definitely the best
mentor ever. I wonder, if I were a chicken,
where in the show would I appear?

I'm pondering the chicken's fate when I notice a second note from Zac: "I've hung a repair kit on the nail next to the curtain in the wing on stage left."

Whoa—this is a scavenger hunt? I sneak to the wing by the curtain (tricky because Dorothy and the Munchkins are dancing there). I only see a roll of duct tape with a Zac tag on it: "Repair kit: If it can't be fixed with duct tape, it's too big a problem for the stage manager." On the back the tag says, "We stage managers have to stick together."

This is WAY COOL.

Just call me the fix-every-problem stage manager. I'm feeling rather powerful.

A minute later I'm called to the costume department to help. It must be important—they asked for me by name. In a minute I find out why: they want me to help with costume fitting.

(I'm feeling a little less powerful now.)

Bleah. I don't
know this costume lady.
All I know is she's a teacher for one of the younger
grades and she is super bossy. I'm not letting it
wreck my good mood.

Mrs. Plassid must have also heard I have "nothing" to do because she breezes in, sees me posing as a tree, gives me a to-do list, and leaves.

To-do:

- Double-check props. Make a list of what we still need.
- Memorize all lines and cues so you can alert all actors five minutes before their stage entrance.
- Keep sharing your good ideas with the director.
- Get used to wearing and using the radio headset. It's part of your stage uniform.
- Double-check costumes. What's done? What's needed? The costume crew made an extra monkey costume by mistake—I hope it's not in place of a costume we really need.
- Have fun!

FINALLY the teacher lets me out of the tree suit. I find Yasmeen and pull her to the school library, to the farthest corner behind the stacks where we can talk privately. I plead with her. "HELP ME!"

Yasmeen doesn't need me to explain. We FOES can practically read each others' minds.

Yasmeen: Have you tried talking to Mo?

Me: Yes, a million times. She won't listen.

Yasmeen: Have you tried calling her?

Me: Once. She never called me back.

Yasmeen gives me the stink eye.

Yasmeen: Have you tried leaving a note?

Me: No. I don't know what to say to her anymore! It started as a crack between us and now it's the Grand Canyon! How do I bridge THAT?

Yasmeen: Say you're SORRY. Mo can't read your mind, you know.

Suddenly I am on a mission: apologize to Mo. I wait for the perfect chance and it never comes.

When rehearsal ends we gather for the Watson Center backstage theater tour that Dad arranged. As we walk up the steps of the theater Dad points out the cornerstone. It says 1912. This place is OLD.

Our tour guide, Renita, meets us in the mezzanine level (the balcony). Everything is ornate—fancy chandeliers hang from the ceiling.

We walk through hallways with framed posters of all the shows from the theater's history (hundreds).

Before going backstage we're warned not to whistle or clap or bring in a mirror, real flowers, or a cat. Renita says those things are seriously bad luck. Yikes.

Everything is painted black. Overhead is a spiderweb of poles and light fixtures. Under our feet is a maze of taped arrows and lines to show the actors where to stand and to show the stagehand—the grip—where to put the scenery. I tell Mo this tour is gripping. She doesn't laugh, but Daquon and Yasmeen do.

We learn the parts of the stage:

We get to stand on the apron and look out into the audience. It's not hard to imagine a huge audience that has come to see us perform. Renita turns on the spotlights. My heart is racing. I start to imagine myself in our play—maybe I really could be a flying monkey. But I shake myself out of that daydream. I can't be stage manager AND an actor. I'm happy to be in the wings instead of wearing them!

When we tour the dressing rooms a bunch of us rush to sit down at the makeup mirrors. I think we're all pretending we're Broadway stars. Renita switches on the rows of lights. They're super bright. I notice Mo's reflection in the mirror—she's looking at me. I smile but she looks away quickly.

I'm relieved when Yasmeen pulls me over to admire the rows of costumes and accessories.

Sequins, fur, satin, velvet—they're fabulous!

Renita takes us to the orchestra level of the theater and tells us to have a seat. I carefully arrange where I stand so I will be able to sit behind Mo.

I lean forward in my chair and whisper, "I'm sorry." Mo doesn't react. Maybe she didn't hear me.

"I'm sorry!" I say it louder. Nothing.

I'm thinking about yelling it when the house lights dim. Everyone hushes. A spotlight finds a guy on stage. It's my mentor, Zac! He announces that all the mentors have been practicing for weeks and they want to show us some of the singing and dancing they'll be performing in a musical show next month.

It's awesome. All of us applaud wildly.

After thanking Renita for the tour, we head outside.

When everyone leaves Dad tells me he scored two tickets to tonight's Watson concert. I'm thinking he and Mom will have a nice time, but he says I get to go!

First we go to dinner at one of the cafeterias at the university.

I love eating on campus. It makes me feel like I'm a student there (a few years early). Everyone is especially nice to me. Plus the food is DELICIOUS (and there's no fungus or toenail clippings).

I'm biting into the best sushi ever when sports coach Dad drops this painful truth: "You and Mo aren't much of a team anymore."

Me: I—uh—yeah.

Dad: What have you tried?

Me: I've tried EVERYTHING. Today I told her I was sorry. No reaction. The worst part is, it's affecting her in the play. Instead of a wicked witch she's a sad one, and I don't know what to do about that.

Dad: How many people are involved in the play?

Me: You mean both cast and crew? I think it's 63, not including teachers.

Dad: How important is each person? Any bench warmers or junk players among them?

Me: Mrs. Plassid says there are no small roles. Every person is important to the success of the show.

Dad: Does Mo understand she's an impact player?

Me: Why wouldn't she understand that? She plays sports. She knows every player matters.

Dad: She knows. But maybe she doesn't remember that she knows. Even all-star players need coaches.

As Dad and I walk to the Watson Center I am thinking about how I can coach Mo.

My thoughts are interrupted by people who seem to come out of the bushes to shake Dad's hand. He knows EVERYONE on campus!

They're all smiling and saying nice things.

I tell Dad he should have his photo on the actors' wall with the other big stage stars. He says everyone's happy because his team happens to be in a winning streak, but the real proof of friendship is how they treat you when your team is losing.

We find our seats (third row!). On the stage
three tall guys and a short guy joke around and
perform some songs I know and loads of songs I like.

Suddenly we hear loud organ music—it sounds
like it doesn't belong. The guys on stage stop
singing. People in the audience are talking—nobody
talks during concerts! We hear a loud laugh,
"Mwahahahaha!"

I clutch Dad's arm. This is freaky!

Something enormous rises from the smoke in the front of the stage. Dad says it's a Wurlitzer pipe organ. A black-caped phantom-type guy is playing it and laughing and yelling at the guys on stage. They call back some funny insults, and I realize this is definitely planned. It's all part of the show.

The audience cheers when the short guy challenges the phantom to a music contest— and wins.

I get all their autographs after the show. We talk about what fun it was at home late into the night—and again at breakfast the next day.

Before school starts I walk Henry, and I'm humming songs from last night.

I watch carefully for squirrels. We see an opossum but it hisses at us and Henry backs up. For the rest of our walk Henry stays on the leash, walking at my side like a good dog (for once).

Thank goodness Mrs. Hamilton isn't outside. Her flowers are still a mess. That couldn't all be from Henry and me, could it?

In school our teachers tie lessons into the play.
Like in Mr. Brendall's science class we study animal
actors who outsmart predators in strange ways.

 ← Opossums fake their death by lying
still when a predator comes near.

Hognose snakes do too! →
(They even bleed a little.)

 ← Vampire squid turn inside out to show off
lots of harmless spikes. Their fake eyes
shrink so it looks like they are swimming
away. Plus they shoot out weird fireworks
that confuse predators.

Leaf insects and walking
sticks look like plant parts. →

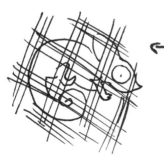 ← Chameleons change colors to match their
background. That's like changing clothes
to match your desk in school.

Other fakes found in my own school hallways:

Jamian fakes out his friends by inventing →
bizarre Oz trivia, hoping they will believe it.

Jamian: To film the Oz tornado,
the director had to lure a tornado
onto the movie set by offering it
big trucks and livestock.
   The rest of us: Wait, WHAT?

← Travis and Sitka like each
other but don't want people
to know yet (except their
closest friends).

Ellie McDoodle pretends everything is →
okay between her and Mo, but really
she's bummed. And she can't figure out
how to make things better.

After science class I ask Travis to help me think up a FOES club handshake. I'm hoping this will be a sort of team builder, bringing Mo and me closer together.

Travis and I come up with this:

1. Stand in a circle. Wave your right hand in an arc from left to right.

2. Spell out FOES with right hand in sign language:

3. Knock knuckles together.
4. In slow motion, spread fingers like fireworks and say "wha-a-a."
5. Jazz hand. (Shake hand back and forth at the wrist.)
6. Put hands in center. Say "FOES!" and lift hands.

We teach it to the rest of the FOES and practice it until we all have it memorized. We are so COOL.

In art class Ms. Trebuchet shows us a slide show of masks. She went to a big museum in New York City, saw these masks, and drew them right there on the spot, with people around her watching. I want to go to that museum soon (with a sketch journal, but without a crowd).

I'm sketching her mask drawings as fast as I can.

Now for the assignment: create a mask of our favorite <u>Wizard of Oz</u> character. My favorite has always been Dorothy. I know it makes no sense, but liking Dorothy seems somehow disloyal to Mo (who still doesn't like me). Maybe I'll do a witch mask instead.

At the end of art class I scrawl a fast message that I hope will make Mo want to talk to me:

Somebody left this on the broom
Of the best actor in the room.

I tape the note to Mo's broom and hide behind the prop room door. I want to see Mo's reaction. I hold my breath when she finally comes into the room. Mo reaches for her broom, pulls off the note, reads it, wads it up, and throws it into the props box. I jump out and block the doorway.

Me: Mo, we HAVE to talk!

Mo: What's there to talk about? You promised me something important and then took it away.

Me: I tried! I argued with the teachers, but they made us give it to Nikki! I wish Nikki would just—just—*disappear in a tornado*!

Mo shakes her head and points behind me.

I turn around to see what Mo's pointing at. Nikki is standing behind me. She looks horrified. Mo is scowling. Then <u>Sitka</u> comes into the hallway.

Are you okay, Mo?

I'm sure Mrs. Plassid heard me on the headset. I slide out the door past them like a jellyfish, like I have no backbone. I want to go home, but instead I go to the last row of seats in the auditorium. I don't know why I bother trying to hide there. I can hear Mrs. Plassid calling for me.

Where's Ellie? Ellie!

Good job. I'm so proud of me. Today I made the fight with Mo WORSE, and I started a NEW fight with Nikki.

My favorite part of the day is always rehearsal. Today it feels like torture.

Mrs. Plassid makes me come to the stage. I have to take notes on what she says. I don't have a choice. Mo and Nikki are giving me dirty looks the whole time.

I wish a tornado would carry ME away.

The show must go on, right? Why?

I can't think about bad stuff. I have to concentrate on what Mrs. Plassid is telling the cast.

My notes:

1. Make your character your own. Add gestures and facial expressions so it isn't a copy of the character in the book or film.
2. If someone makes a mistake on stage, ignore it.
3. If it's a <u>big</u> mistake, say something to help the blunder make sense to the audience and to help get the play back on track.

I stop taking notes and look at her. Is she serious? Is she saying we should ignore the script onstage?

As if she read my mind, Mrs. Plassid says the best thing would be to just stick to the script and ignore mistakes. Good. I hope everyone remembers that.

During the break I tell Yasmeen about the note I put on Mo's broom to make her feel good, and how it backfired.

Yasmeen: Try again.

Me: No. I tried. It didn't work. I give up.

At the end of rehearsal Mrs. Plassid always gathers us for a closing ring. We cross arms and join hands while she says nice things about how the day went. She sends around the squeeze, sort of a hand hug. She squeezes my hand, I squeeze the next person's hand, and if you watch you'll see the grip go around the circle, until it comes back to Mrs. Plassid.

I usually stand with the FOES. Today I grab Travis's and Daquon's hands and hold tight.

Mo leaves with Sitka.

Before Nikki leaves I suck up all my courage and ask her if we can talk. She says yes. Major relief. I pull her off to the side where we won't get interrupted. I apologize for what I said earlier, about wanting a tornado to take her away.

I tell her I only said it because I was frustrated and trying to patch up a fight with Mo.

Amazingly, Nikki says she understands. She says it's a little funny that I was wishing a tornado would carry her off since she's Dorothy. She even hugs me. I wish it were this easy to get Mo to see my side of things. I head home feeling a little better.

At home after dinner Risa works on her school's All Arts Faux Show. Faux means fake, Risa tells me. (It's pronounced "foe.") The show will be all sorts of fake discoveries, and the rock she is making is now a mermaid "fossil." I want her to make me one!

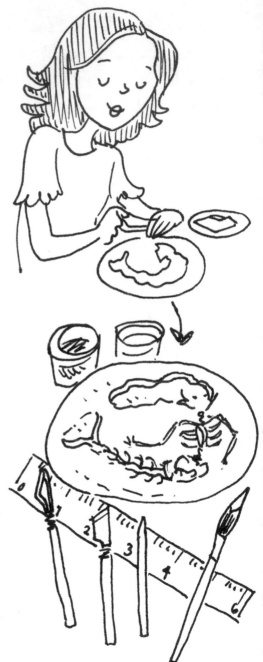

She says I should bring my friends to the show.

I doubt Mo wants to be anywhere near me, but the rest of the FOES might come. I'll ask them tomorrow.

Meanwhile, Josh helps me make my robot for school. Mostly I watch him and hand him old toy parts. Actually, mostly I watch Risa. The little mermaid she's making is so cute! Josh keeps reminding me to pay attention. He says he wishes he had more time to work on this. It's due tomorrow, though.

I call it FrankenRobot.

recorded voice

teeth open and close

clock heartbeat

magnetic hands move how?

remote-controlled base

The next morning I get to school early with
FrankenRobot. Most of the others are cool art
sculptures, but some are amazing!! I'm quite
sure they cost a ton of money to make, and I am
positive they weren't made by sixth graders alone.
  This makes me feel a little better about my robot.

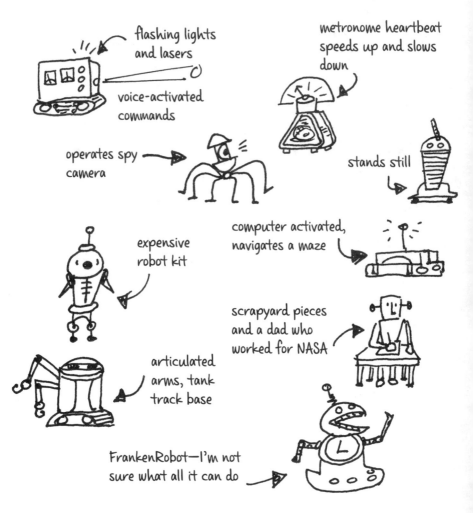

flashing lights
and lasers

voice-activated
commands

metronome heartbeat
speeds up and slows
down

operates spy
camera

stands still

expensive
robot kit

computer activated,
navigates a maze

scrapyard pieces
and a dad who
worked for NASA

articulated
arms, tank
track base

FrankenRobot—I'm not
sure what all it can do

I felt a little guilty since it's mostly Josh's work. But I'm busy with so many things for the play. I don't have time to do super-fancy, extra-involved work right now. Besides, I _did_ help with it.

Okay, I probably should have paid more attention to Josh and less to Risa's mermaid. But the mermaid is adorable!!! It looks real! Anyway, on the next project I'll do better.

At lunch when Sitka leaves our table to talk to Mrs. Plassid about her Good Witch costume, I want to ask the FOES to come to the Faux Show. Instead Travis asks if we can make Sitka one of the FOES.

I'm <u>totally</u> against that.

The group is fine the way it is right now. I don't like how Sitka is pulling Mo away from me. Maybe I'm jealous. I don't want to actually say how I feel to the group, though. I'm pretty sure everyone else thinks we should let Sitka into the FOES.

I try to sound casual:

How could we call ourselves the Five of Epic Sagacity if there are six of us? How would our handshake work with six instead of five? With two guys and four girls, will our group be too unbalanced? What if we decide later we made a mistake? What if we want to add more people? Should we have some rules written down for this sort of thing?

I see the time.
I stall
by asking
more questions.
Finally,
RINGGG!

Oh, there's the bell! Gotta run!

Travis is the first to catch up with me. "Ellie, wow, that was heartless. You know the handshake works with any number of people."

Before I have a chance to answer, Daquon joins him. "That wasn't your smartest move."

Yasmeen looks like she's about to pile on and add to my misery. "Ellie—"

I don't want to hear it. Cheezers. Can't I do anything right? I mumble an apology and go to class.

In Mr. Brendall's math class I have too much time to think.

It's not like keeping Sitka out of the group will bring Mo closer to me. I've already lost Mo. I don't want to lose the other FOES. I scribble four copies of this note:

I'm sorry about lunch. I vote yes on Sitka.

PS—Want to go to the art show and concert at the high school tonight? It could be our first new FOES meeting. Check off your answer:
__ yes, sounds like fun!
__ no, but I wish I could
__ maybe

I get back three yeses and a maybe with an extra message: "Only if Sitka can go too." I bet that's from Mo.

In rehearsal we work on makeup. Stage lights brighten shadows so that the actors' faces look flat. Makeup makes them look 3-D again.

We have little palettes for each person—I help scoop colors onto plates. Working from photos, the actors apply their own makeup.

This trivia from Jamian is true: while they were filming the Oz movie, the first Tin Man almost died from the aluminum dust in his makeup. Sitka panics. "Is Travis's makeup dangerous?"

"Theater makeup is different and much safer today. Still, make sure you clean off every speck at the end of the day," says Mrs. Plassid.

The rest of today's rehearsal is pure fun. We make sure all the costumes are complete and everything fits. A photographer comes to take photos for the program booklet, posters, and newspaper articles. I have to admit, the costume crew did an amazing job.

I want my picture taken with the monkeys because I designed their outfits. The monkey actors have extra roles. They're Munchkins and Emerald City people too. That's three costume and makeup changes.

All crew members wear the same costume as me: all black. It's not exciting or flashy, but we blend into the stage background perfectly.

I notice Daquon and Travis are whispering a lot. When Mrs. Plassid sends everyone to change out of costumes and makeup, I find out why. Scarecrow and Tin Man link elbows with me and skip, steering me to the back of the auditorium. It's so goofy, I laugh.

Daquon and Travis at the same time: Can we talk?

Me: Sure. What's up?

Travis: Ellie, you're a good person.

Daquon: You have a lot of friends. A lot of cool people like you.

Travis: We're watching you try to patch up this problem with Mo, and we feel bad for you.

Me: (Nothing. I keep swallowing, hoping it'll make my throat stop hurting. It doesn't.)

Daquon: We've known Mo a long time. We think there's a 98% chance she'll come back to you.

Me: I want a 100% chance.

Travis: What if that's impossible?

Daquon: My mom says you can be the best strawberry ever, and you will still find people who don't like strawberries.

Me: Wait, what? Strawberries?

Travis: What that means is, not everyone is going to love you or be your best friend. That's life. You get good stuff and you get bad stuff.

Daquon: If you lose Mo completely, I promise that something else even better will come next. And if I'm wrong you can—what?

Travis: You can make him dance the hula in front of the whole school. With a chicken.

Daquon: And you can make Travis join in.

Ha! That I'd like to see.

When we walk back to rehearsal, Mrs. Plassid reminds us tomorrow is the deadline to submit any art for the program booklet cover. I'd completely forgotten! On the way home I try to think of a good idea for it, but my brain is too full of what Daquon and Travis said—and hula dancing with chickens.

At home I don't have time to draw covers. Mom makes us eat fast and then whisks us all off to the high school's Faux Show: Things Aren't As They Seem.

I sit with the FOES—all six of us in a row. First the orchestra (with Risa, Josh, and Peter) performs songs from our play. I like watching the conductor, Mr. Cornelius.

He jabs his baton—wiggling, twisting, bending, almost dancing. It's funny.

The music for the tornado is surprisingly scary. Daquon whispers, "I expect to see a cow go flying."

"And a truck!" says Yasmeen.

It's hard to giggle silently.

After the concert the FOES visit the art gallery.

Risa's MERmaid fossil, "found by NASA's Mars Exploration Rover." (These little cards give fake details.)

Tiny dead sprite encased in amber tree sap. It's creepy and sweet at the same time. →

I notice Mo laughing at Ben-Ben the dog, who LOVES the attention.

Tip and cross section of a unicorn's horn. It has a blunt tip from scratching it on rocks. The card says the number of ring ridges is the unicorn's age in years. That part is the "Sparkle Sac," which is a small gland found behind a unicorn's left ear.

The FOES actually have a lot of fun at this show. Let me make this clear: I'm not happy about this new reality of Mo being a friend but not my best friend. Still, if I can't change it, I guess I have to accept it.

Returning home from the Faux Show I hardly have any time to throw together something for the program booklet. I end up looking at art from the original Oz books for inspiration.

Maybe I should I have put more into my art, but I mostly did my best. I'm especially proud of my signature, which took a LONG time to perfect. I'm really hoping Mrs. Plassid lets me redraw the program cover before sending it to the printer. I think I could improve it if I drew it a second time.

I turn in my art first thing in the morning. I also include a few new sketches on the back, in case Mrs. Plassid wants to use one of them instead.

Next I head to art class, where we're finishing our masks.

Because I usually finish my art projects faster than my friends do, I have time to doodle. I'm playing with my new signature with the star over the "i."

Daquon: Did you know doodling can change your emotion? If you see something disturbing and then draw happy doodles, you actually feel happier.

Yasmeen: What's a happy doodle?

Me: I would guess smiley faces, hearts, stars, and rainbows.

Travis: And unicorn sparkle sacs!

Sitka: For my little sister, happy doodles are skulls and explosions. She likes pirate-y stuff.

Ms. Trebuchet stops by our table and asks: Do masks change our emotions or just hide them?

We decide they can do both.

Travis: Wearing a scary Halloween mask, I feel more powerful.

Mo: When I wear fancy clothes it makes me act more proper. That's part of why I didn't want the witch role. I don't want to act like a mean person.

Me: But—the villain is vital! Without bad, how can you identify good? If Dorothy has an easy time getting home, the ending isn't satisfying.

Mo: I hadn't thought about that.

Maybe Mo sees things differently now, but I'm not crazy enough to think it'll fix the problems in our friendship. She said she didn't want to act like a mean person. But I feel she's been mean to me!

It doesn't matter. I have more important things to think about. Like, the high school orchestra visits for rehearsal, and we'll run through the entire Oz production with music (without costumes).

The front of the stage lowers to make an orchestra pit for all the musicians.

Josh on tuba

Peter on cello
Risa on flute

I'm watching from the back row of the auditorium

At the end Mrs. Plassid calls our show spectacular. I agree! Too soon it's time to go home.

After dinner Risa sets up a craft. She's making paper flowers. She says I'll feel happy if I help her. I'm thinking <u>she</u> will feel happy if I help her. I help anyway.

How to Make a Flower:

1. Start with a square of newspaper, 3 x 3 inches.

2. Fold it in half.

3. Fold it in half again.

4. Fold into a triangle.

5. Draw a petal pattern on it.

6. Cut the shaded part off.

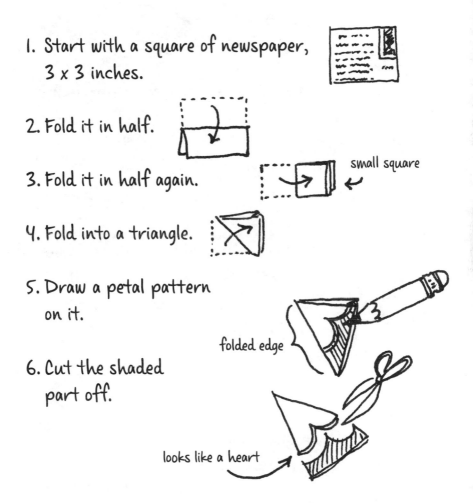

small square

folded edge

looks like a heart

7. Unfold.

8. Cut out one petal section.

9. Glue part A onto part B.

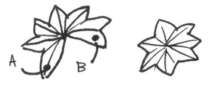

A   B

10. When it's dry, stick a pipe cleaner through it
for a stem.

Variations: Make different sizes. Glue
buttons in the centers. Put smaller
flowers inside larger ones. Color with
markers. Curl the petal
edges around a pencil.

I make a zillion flowers. Risa has
way more than she needs so she gives
me the extras. I have a plan for them.

On the way to school the next morning I sneak over to Mrs. Hamilton's house. Her flower bed is still looking trampled. I'm like a spy. I look around carefully. I wipe beads of sweat off my brow. It's a quiet mission of kindness. I put the vase on the porch and start to ring the bell.

I hear a muffled voice shouting something. A fist beats on the window near the porch. It scares me so much I jump six feet into the air.

It's Mrs. Hamilton. I point to the porch. She can't see the flowers I put there. She cranks open the window and yells, "Haven't you done enough here? Get off my property. Rotten kids!"

I could stop and explain, but I'd rather run like a scared rabbit.

At school I'm all sweaty, thanks to Mrs. Hamilton. I HATE being misunderstood. She's a witch. I swear it.

During silent reading I stew. Travis notices I'm upset. He signs to me: U—O—K?

My heart melts. I sign to him: M-R-S H-A-M-I-L-T-O-N-S E-V-I-L.

Travis signs: F-O-E-S M-E-E-T-I-N-G.

U   O   K

It's sweet that he's worried about me. No wonder Sitka likes him. I nod yes and sign T-H-X for thanks.

A FOES meeting is exactly what I need!

T   H   X

Mrs. Whittam calls our English class to order and tells us to work on our Oz film scenes while she hands out papers with our robot grades.

My scene: An army of monkeys grabs Dorothy and Toto and takes them to the witch's castle.

I have <u>nothing</u> for it yet, and I'm still upset about Mrs. Hamilton's meanness, so I draw. That always calms me down. I can work on my scene later.

Mrs. Hamilton

A voice comes over the speaker in our classroom. It's Mrs. Plassid. She sounds really happy.

"And the winner of the cover contest is . . ."

I brace myself and smile.

"Will Denslow!"

Wait.

No.

I am in total shock. Will is throwing his hands up, acting like he scored a touchdown. Some people stare at me. Everybody congratulates him.

This is the biggest thing I wanted this week, to have my art on the cover of the show program book.

How did I blow it? Why isn't that me celebrating and high-fiving everyone? I feel numb.

Ignoring my pain, Mrs. Whittam gives me my robot paper with no grade on it. It only says, "See me."

Figuring she's going to give me extra credit for such an awesome robot, I go to Mrs. Whittam's desk and hold up my paper for her to see.

Mrs. Whittam: Did you do the work on your robot, or did someone else?

Me: I did some of it. My brother helped me.

Mrs. Whittam: Draw me a pie chart showing how much your brother helped and how much was your work.

I swear I am going to throw up, right here in class.

I draw this:

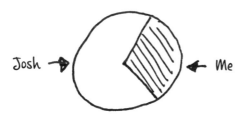 

Mrs. Whittam: That's what I thought.

She takes back the paper and writes a D on it. She hands it to me, frowning. I stumble back to my seat.

Can this class get any worse? Yes, it can and it does. Mrs. Whittam announces we only have through the weekend to finish our Oz scene.

I think my head is going to explode. I can't be creative when I'm feeling rotten! I wrack my brain for some spark of a creative idea for my scene, but I don't have any. I'm going to have to work on this at home tonight and all weekend. Yippee.

This is the worst day of my life. I want to go home.

Me: This is so wrong. I should have won that contest.

Yasmeen: Ellie, do you realize who you sound like? Now do you understand how Mo felt?

Me: What? That doesn't help me at all! This is completely different! You know what? Forget it.

I don't want to talk about it. They don't understand. For the rest of the day I am quiet. No conversations and no laughing. I'm a wisp, not a person. The FOES surround me and try to make me laugh by telling dumb jokes.

What's the opposite of a cat?

An inside-out cat!

I refuse to smile.

Finally, the last bell of the day rings. Travis asks about the FOES meeting after school. I just shake my head no. It's officially the weekend. Good-bye, school.

There's no place like home.

At home I can think. I don't want to take a chance of letting Josh do my project, so I hide in my room to work on it. I put on my best music and let my pet rat, Ophelia, help me brainstorm. I make lists of ideas.

It takes a while, but eventually the brainstorming pays off. Good ideas start to flow. I write down every little thing that comes to mind. One of them will work.

> An army of monkeys grabs Dorothy and Toto and takes them to the witch's castle.

This is what I come up with for my scene:

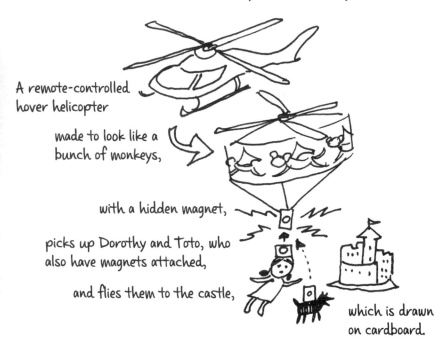

A remote-controlled hover helicopter

made to look like a bunch of monkeys,

with a hidden magnet,

picks up Dorothy and Toto, who also have magnets attached,

and flies them to the castle,

which is drawn on cardboard.

It's impressive but not crazy complicated.

My family's involved, even though they don't know it:

I use Mom's art supplies and Josh's helicopter toy. The monkeys look like Ben-Ben. The voice in my head that keeps telling me to work fast and get the job done is like Risa's. There's a coach in my head too, and it's telling me I'm acing this. That's Dad's voice. Everyone stops in to see how I am doing, but I keep working.

I thought I would dread this time, but I am glad to have a whole weekend off. No school. No drama. It's time to make this project the best it can be.

I practice getting the monkey-copter to hover, lift, and fly. It's PERFECT. I can't wait to show it off.

When Monday comes I walk confidently into English class. We perform our scenes. Mrs. Whittam films each one. She'll edit them all together and make copies for all of us later. Cheezers. It's a little scary knowing your work will live on in film long after you made it.

There are some minor glitches in some of the presentations, but it's just about the best two hours ever, and I'm proud of my part in it.

All of the FOES do a fantastic job.

I'm floating I'm so happy. Then Tech Week starts.

Tech Week is the last week of the play, filled with intense rehearsals. We're making sure everything runs smoothly, the music is flawless, the lights and sound happen when and where they should, and there are no problems with anything in the show.

We go through the entire play, and it's mostly great. Still, there are definitely some things to work out.

For one thing, Toto goes all junkyard dog, snapping at Dorothy. Or, as Daquon says, Toto embraces his inner lions and tigers and bears.

Mrs. Plassid removes Toto from the show.

"We'll use a toy instead," she says.

I cannot believe my ears.

"Nooo!" I argue with Mrs. Plassid.

"Toto is the show's hero! He is why Dorothy's late getting into the storm cellar. He pulls back the curtain to reveal the bad wizard. He makes Dorothy miss the balloon escape near the end. Because of that, she has to use the magic slippers to get home.

"Toto can't be a toy."

I'm on the ground, begging. I know it's dramatic, but I can't help it. I really believe in what I'm saying.

I ask if anyone knows a real dog who is small and really cool. (My dog, Henry, is way too big and too stubborn.)

I'm shocked when Mo suggests Ben-Ben as Toto: "At the Faux Art Show he was the perfect faux dog."

Mrs. Plassid says, "Let's try it."

I call Mom.

That night Risa helps me invent a new, mostly healthy doggie treat for Ben-Ben.

We call it Toto Mix. It's a scoop of every kind of cereal in our pantry plus raisins, nuts, seeds, and a few little pieces of chocolate.

Ben-Ben thinks the mix is candy. We tell him this is a game. When he does something right, he gets a treat.

If he gets lots of treats, he can be a dog for the whole school. He wags his tail so hard he falls over sideways. And he licks my face. Disgusting.

Me: Sit! Good boy!
Ben-Ben: Grrrr!
Me: Oops, sorry!
I mean, good dog!
Ben-Ben: Arf!

Next we teach Ben-Ben about his part in the play.

I think on a leash he'll be a fantastic stage dog.

Toto needs a costume. I tell Mom we can work with the extra flying monkey costume, but she says we need thick, long fur for a believable Toto. She whips up a costume overnight!

The next day, dress rehearsal is perfect. Mrs. Plassid calls Ben-Ben a hardworking genius on stage (he's a much better dog than hers). He remembers his lines and does everything exactly right. I think his favorite part is barking at Cowardly Lion.

Woof, woof!

The next three days are a blur of rehearsals.
Our teachers hold back on homework assignments.
While the sixth grade is working on the play, it
seems the rest of the school gets Oz fever. All
the classes decorate the hallways with art and
writing. A yellow brick road made of paper winds
through the halls. Everybody is super excited
about the play.

Mrs. Plassid adds to my list of responsibilities: now I'm also welcoming the audience and introducing the show! She gives me a list of what to say, but she lets me decide how to say it. I want to be the best play introducer ever.

I come up with a surprise for the cast. I will need that extra monkey costume after all.

The big day arrives and I think we're ready for it. It's almost showtime! I can't wait!

At home in the morning I go over Ben-Ben's role on stage:
1. Don't pull the leash.
2. Obey Dorothy.
3. Keep the costume on during the whole play.

At school, we try to concentrate on our class work, but it's impossible!

After school we go home for a quick dinner. Dad has cooked up some homemade pizza, but I'm too nervous to eat much.

When it's time, we rush to school.

It's thrilling to see everyone in costume and makeup. This is it. Finally. Our show. Some are reading the script, making sure they remember their lines completely. I could recite the whole play backward I know it so well.

I hug Mom and Dad. I see Zac! He tells me to remember to enjoy this because opening night only happens once. And he says "Break a leg!" which means "Have an awesome show!"

I get ready for my introduction. Peering through the curtains, I see the auditorium fill with people. The orchestra and actors take their places. The house lights darken. That's my cue.

Yikes. I step into the spotlight and survey the audience. In the shadow behind the conductor— is that . . . ? I squint. Yes. It's Mrs. Hamilton! Double yikes. Suddenly what I am about to say takes on extra significance. Yoga-breathing time. Push back the fear. Smile and start.

"Welcome to our sixth grade play, <u>The Wizard of Oz</u>. My green boss lady demands that you turn off your cell phones so they don't interfere with her crystal ball. Now we begin the story of a wicked little girl who terrorizes a nice old lady." (The audience laughs. Yay!)

Yes, I am dressed in the monkey costume. I take the hood off when I get backstage.

The curtain opens. The play begins. In the first scene, Dorothy and Toto are racing home from the evil neighbor's garden.

Nikki sings her rainbow song. I see her parents filming it in the audience. Her grandma is wiping tears. Aw!

Mo as Miss Gulch threatens Toto, so Dorothy and Toto run away.

A tornado takes Dorothy to Munchkinland. I'm excited to see my yellow brick road idea work— the illusion is fantastic!

Dorothy enrages the Wicked Witch of the West and is given the red cowboy boots (our twist on ruby slippers).

Dorothy heads out on the yellow brick road to the Emerald City, hoping the Wizard will help her get home to Kansas. Ben-Ben barks at all the right times. Nikki gives him treats from her basket.

Daquon dances his Scarecrow jig and sings.

The enchanted apple trees throw apples at Dorothy.

One apple bounces into the forest, and Travis as the Tin Man enters the story. I love his steampunk costume.

Suddenly there's a problem backstage! I give Ryan his five-minute cue and discover our Cowardly Lion is afraid to go on stage.

Me: You ruled the stage at auditions!

(He smiles a little, for a second.)

Me: You can do this. You're the best lion of the whole school.

Ryan: No, I've been faking it.

Me: Brave doesn't mean fearless. It means you do what you need to do even if you're afraid. Plus it's okay to fake it until you feel it. If you're scared on stage, it'll look like you're a really good actor.

Ryan: Okay, maybe you're right.

He steps onto the stage without missing his first line. I cheer silently. Mrs. Plassid whispers over the headset: "Excellent, Ellie!"

I'm quietly patting myself on the back when everything suddenly gets much worse.

Ryan's on stage and he's supposed to sing. The music swells. We've practiced this a hundred times. No sound comes out of Ryan.

The orchestra plays the intro again. Nothing.

Maybe he forgot the words.

I whisper the first line. There's no reaction.

Maybe he didn't hear me. I whisper louder.

And then singing starts, but he isn't moving his lips.

It's like a miracle. Like the clouds opened and a song poured out.

My eyes scan the stage. Nobody on the stage is saying a word. Where's it coming from?

The song comes from
backstage. Somebody
behind the curtains
is singing.

Ryan looks just as
confused as I am.

Halfway through the
second line, he joins
the song, sort of. He's not
singing loud enough, but
the powerful backstage
voice carries it.

Suddenly I know whose
voice it is. It's Mo.

She's singing Ryan's
song.

Or, rather, she's
howling it.

She's way off-key.
It's perfect—because
it sounds like a lion in
real pain should.

I watch with my
mouth open.

Ryan and Mo finish his song together.

I see tears on Ryan's cheeks—are they real?

Nikki/Dorothy hugs him. That part isn't in the script, but it's sweet and it fits.

Ryan loosens up. He wipes his face with his tail. Then he, Nikki/Dorothy, Travis/Tin Man, and Daquon/Scarecrow link elbows and dance down the yellow brick road, singing loudly. This time Ryan's singing too.

Ben-Ben keeps pace, barking in tune. It's <u>SO</u> cute.

The audience bursts into loud applause. Whew!!!

In the wings across the stage from me, where nobody but I can see her, Mrs. Plassid waves jazz hands. I know that means she's extremely happy at what just happened. So am I!

The play continues.

The four travelers journey through strange lands and meet weird characters like the Kalidahs (monster tiger-bears that are in the Oz books and our show, but not the movie).

Dorothy and her friends arrive at the Emerald City. Ryan-Lion sings again, this time by himself.

The audience LOVES him.

Jamian as the Wizard makes his big entrance. In our show he's a blustery hot-air balloonist, dressed for a quick getaway.

The Wizard gives Dorothy and her friends an almost-impossible task: bring him the Wicked Witch's broomstick and he'll grant her request.

Dorothy wants to go home. Scarecrow wants a brain. Tin Man wants a heart. Lion wants courage. Ben-Ben/Toto wants a treat. He's terrific on stage, so Dorothy gives him one.

In the greenroom, the cast waiting room, everyone can hear the play over the loudspeakers. I give Mo, the monkeys, and the Winkie soldiers their cue:

Five minutes: Witch, flying monkeys, and Winkies.

Mo jumps up.

When she stands, her witch costume catches in the hinge of the folding chair and RIPS!! She walks quickly to the stage. <u>Nobody</u> notices except me!

Instant replay: Mo's dress catches and RIPS!!!

I follow her to the edge of the stage.

Mo—wait!

She rushes past me. She doesn't hear me. (Well, I don't say it out loud! We're right next to the stage!)

I can't let her go on stage with a ripped dress. Everyone will see her underwear. They'll make fun of her forever.

All in one motion I grab a monkey suit, put it half on, pull the duct tape off the nail, follow Mo, and lock eyes with Sitka. She shakes her head and tries to stop me.

"Don't!!" she whispers. "It's no big deal! Mrs. Plassid said to ignore mistakes!"

I ignore Sitka. Cheezers! I HAVE to protect Mo.
I burst through the curtain onto the stage.

Let me rephrase that. I FOLLOW MO OUT ONTO
THE STAGE IN FRONT OF A MILLION PEOPLE!!!
IN A HALF-PUT-ON MONKEY HOOD!!!

I rip off a length of duct tape. I smack it
across her rip. Then I run offstage and hide
in the wings, where I am supposed to stay,
where I can see everything but the audience
can't see me.

Maybe with all the monkeys on stage in that
scene, nobody will notice what I did.

At this point I almost
pass out. I can't believe
what just happened.

I shake it off and avoid
Mrs. Plassid's eyes. In fact,
I avoid EVERYONE'S eyes.

Onstage, Mo says,
"You monkeys drive
me bananas!"

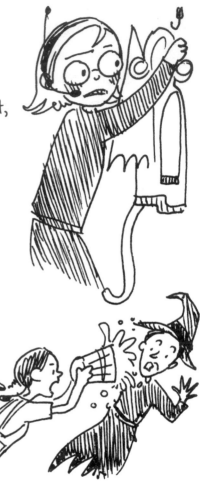

The audience laughs.
The play continues.

I watch with my heart
pounding so loud it drowns
out the bass drum in the
orchestra. When Nikki
throws water on the
Witch, Mo "melts"
off of the stage.
The audience cheers.

Backstage, Mo stares
at me.

We can't talk, though.
I have to cue the Wizard
and Glinda.

Dorothy and her friends take the witch's broomstick to the Wizard.

Ben-Ben gets his big moment in the spotlight when he pulls back the Wizard's curtain with his teeth. The audience cheers again, and he barks at them, which makes them laugh.

Three clicks of Nikki's heels take her home (Toto too!). It was all a dream. Dorothy wakes up in her bed in Kansas.

Personally, I dislike dream endings. I like the <u>Wizard of Oz</u> book's ending more: Dorothy clicks her heels, takes three steps, and lands in Kansas, wide awake.

The audience applauds wildly. I peek out of the curtains. One person in the front row stands up, clapping. More people rise. It's like a wave from the front of the room to the back, and soon the whole audience is standing. This must be what they mean by a standing ovation.

It was started by one person—grouchy old Mrs. Hamilton? That makes no sense. But I have no time to think about it.

Backstage is a hugfest. Everyone's in on it—
the actors, the crew, Mrs. Plassid, the principal,
and even some of the parents. I rub Ben-Ben's
belly and his leg thumps. We only have a minute,
though—we have to run back out onto the stage
for our curtain call.

I wrote the script for the curtain call: first
the Emerald City people bow. Then they put on
their monkey hoods and bow again. Then they take
off the hoods and put on Munchkin hats and
bow AGAIN. People are clapping like crazy now.
The main characters follow, then the crew, the
orchestra, and Mrs. Plassid and I (with no monkey
suit). Getting this much applause is magical.

The actors all walk out to the super-crowded lobby to greet their adoring public. They're immediately swarmed by autograph seekers. A lot of little kids are in Oz costumes. How cute! I wander into the chaos.

One boy holds up a pen and his program booklet to me. I'm inspecting the art on the cover. I like it. I have to admit Will did a better job than I would have. The kid interrupts my thoughts, asking if I'm anyone in the play.

I say no.

He says okay and grabs the pen and program from my hands.

I'm surprised to hear Mo's voice. "Ellie is the stage manager PLUS she's a flying monkey."

The kid wants my autograph now.

I'm embarrassed but kind of glad to sign it (with a star dotting the "i").

"You played a more important role than you thought," Mo continues.

"So did you, Mo," I say. "The role I want is to be your friend."

She says, "You've always been my friend. I miss you."

She hugs me.

I tear up.

After most of the crowd leaves, Mom and Dad ask me and Mo for autographs. We laugh and sign their programs. They see Mo's parents and walk over to talk with them.

Suddenly Mrs. Hamilton is in front of me, smiling. Even when she smiles she looks angry. I feel my peaceful happiness drain right out of me—and all of my energy goes with it. <u>Why</u> is she here? Exhausted from this long day, I stand there, ready to take whatever she hits me with.

Something bumps against my back. It's all five FOES, surrounding me! With Mo's and Sitka's arms around my shoulders, I feel strong.

Mrs. Hamilton lays a fancy bouquet of flowers in my hand. She clasps my other hand in her scary bony fingers, sort of bouncing it slowly for emphasis as she speaks. Plus she stares at me intensely.

I swear this is the longest minute in history. I look down at her hands, up at her face, with my mouth gaping open.

Her: Thank you for the darling paper flowers. I'm sorry for raising my voice at you.

Me: Uh. I. Uh.

Her: Your play was delightful. That was good thinking, with the duct tape on the Witch.

Me: Thanks!

At last Mrs. Hamilton lets go. Sitka hugs me. The FOES and I walk to the dressing rooms to get changed out of costumes and makeup. On the way, Mo gets us skipping and singing like Dorothy and her friends on the yellow brick road. It's sooo goofy. We're all laughing our heads off. I LOVE THE FOES!!! (We're Friends of Epic Sagacity now that there are six of us.)

Everything is going perfectly, but now it feels like this is the end. We have another show tomorrow, and we're tired right now, but nobody wants to let go of tonight. We finally say good night and hug each other and then head to our parents' cars.

Mom and Dad, Risa, Josh, Toto, and I buckle into our seats. Everyone is quiet while Dad drives. I'm thinking how deflating this is, to go home after such an exciting day. I try to cheer myself up by replaying the best parts of today in my head. It only barely works.

Maybe Dad is kind of sad too, because he doesn't seem to be thinking straight. He turns the wrong way and heads downtown. He parks in a big parking lot and turns the car off.

We get out of the car. Wait. Do I know those people? Hey! It's everyone from the play. All the FOES are here. And lots of other families too. We follow the crowd inside a dark door. I'm totally confused.

There's a party inside!!!!!!!!!!!

Nikki's parents rented this hall for us to celebrate our first performance. So, like with <u>The Wizard of Oz</u>, there's a sort of second ending to the story—except this isn't a dream!

I see pizza and a big cake with the art from the program cover on it (Will's looking awfully proud of that) and lots of snacks—all Oz themed.

Risa and Josh and some of their orchestra friends set up a band, and we dance to some jazzed-up versions of the show music. And we let loose!

Ben-Ben doesn't have his costume on anymore, but he's definitely still a dog, and he dances with us. Yasmeen says Ben-Ben needs a Toto tutu.

That brings on LOADS of jokes and goofy riddles.

Q: What does Scarecrow eat?
A: Straw-berries!

Q: What did the Munchkins say when Dorothy said good-bye?
A: "Drop in again sometime!"

Q: What happened when a tornado sucked up Cowardly Lion and Toto?
A: It rained cats and dogs.

Q: Why did Dorothy cry?
A: Because Tin Man stepped on her toetoe.

Q: Why did the onion in the play start to cry?
A: Because the director yelled, "Cut!"

Mo made bracelets for all the FOES.

They all say "Friends," but mine says "Ellie: BEST Friend." She made them last night—before I covered her rip. That's good to know.

I'm thinking about how Dorothy has to leave her good friends and go home to Kansas.

I'm luckier than she is.

Yasmeen: I'll miss the play when it's over.

Daquon: We should start a role-playing game. RPG—it's like acting but with fewer rules.

Mo: Our acting doesn't have to end!

Sitka: End? We still have two more performances!

Travis: The next show will be MUCH easier.

Me: What about the rubber chicken from Zac? Where do we work him in?

Mo: We don't have to decide yet. We have two days.

Daquon: Whatever we come up with, I'm sure it'll be clever as a gizzard. For now, we party!

Daquon starts dancing with Rubber Chickie. We all crack up.

Yasmeen: Tomorrow is Saturday. We have no school and no homework.

Me: Hey! Let's have a FOES meeting at my house. We can have lunch and think about Rubber Chickie's big performance, and maybe start the RPG?

Mo: I love your home, Ellie. There's no place like it.

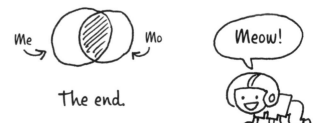

The end.

ACKNOWLEDGMENTS

Special thanks to this behind-the-scenes crew:

Kim Norman, Zac Thompson, Jennifer Barshaw, Jack Barshaw, Brian McNally, Joshua McCune, Diane Allen, Dave Lepard, Johann Wessels, Mary McCafferty Douglas, Erin Murphy, Caroline Abbey, Donna Mark, Melanie Cecka, Ryan Hipp, the cast and crew of the Ellie McDoodle play at the Miller College Children's Theater Project, the casts and crews of All-of-Us-Express Children's Theater, and my family: Charlie, Lisa, Matt, Joe, Caitlin, Katie, Emily, Cayden, Izzy, Sophie, and newborn Addy.

RUTH McNALLY BARSHAW, lifelong cartoonist, writer, and artist, worked in the advertising field, illustrated for newspapers, and won numerous essay-writing contests before becoming the creator of the Ellie McDoodle Diaries. In her spare time she studies martial arts, plays harmonica, and travels—always with a sketch journal. She lives in Lansing, Michigan, with her creative, prank-loving family. See her work at www.ruthexpress.com.